■SCHOLASTIC

Stella and Class:
Information Experts

by Janiel Wagstaff
Illustrated by Dana Regan

For the teachers of the writers and the writers themselves:
explore the magic of writing every single day!
YOU CAN!

ISBN: 978-1-338-26477-7
Copyright © 2018 by Janiel Wagstaff
Illustrations: Dana Regan © Staff Development for Educators
All rights reserved. Printed in the U.S.A.

2 3 4 5 6 7 8 9 10   155   23 22 21 20 19 18

Do you know what it's like to be inquisitive? To have your mind racing with questions? I do.

I'm Stella, grade two.

I wonder about a lot of things, like hot-air balloons. They're beautiful! But, how do those great big things fly?

And gymnastics. How can those gymnasts do so many flip-flop, flip-flop, flip-flops in a row like that? It's dizzying.

I'd like to find out how they do it. Maybe I could flip-flop, too!

And animals...my friends are whacko about animals, and they have a lot of questions about them.

In our class, a boy named Lucas is cheetah-crazy.

He reads EVERYTHING he can about them: books, magazines, web pages...sometimes I think he's gonna' grow whiskers and sprout spots!

So, how about you? You're a kid with an inquiring mind.
What do you have questions about?

Several days ago, our second-grade class was reading a book about chameleons. It was a storybook, but we started asking all kinds of questions about *real* chameleons. Do they actually change color? Why do they have those big, bulgy eyes? Can their eyes really point in two different directions at the same time?

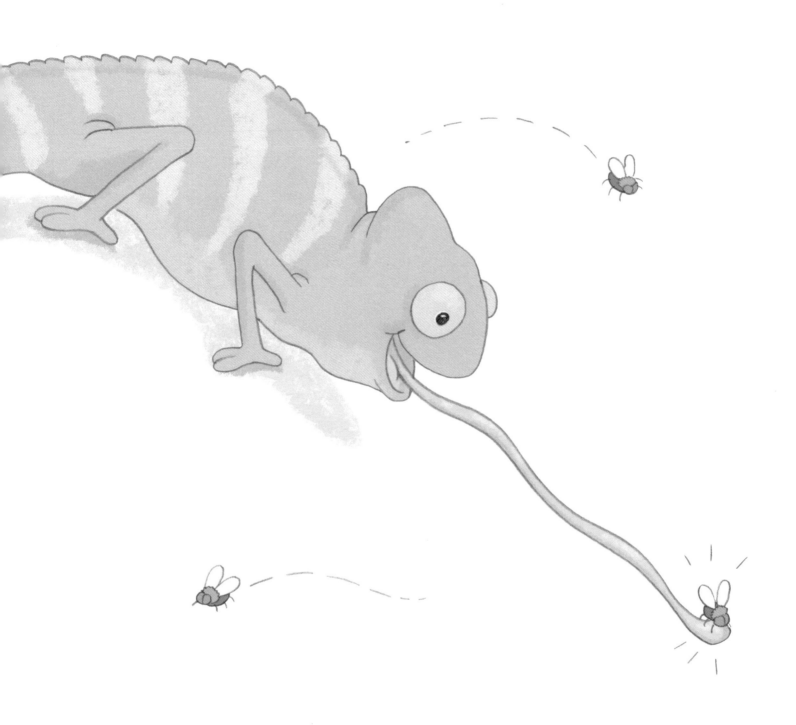

And, how fast are those sticky tongues? I mean, have *you* ever tried to catch a fly? Good luck! But it looks easy for chameleons. Those tongues must be fast as lightning!

Ms. Merkley, our teacher, wrote our questions on a big sheet of paper. She said, "Let's become chameleon experts! We'll answer our questions by reading several sources and checking facts on the internet. We'll jot notes as we learn. Then, we can do some informative writing to share what we find!"

Woohoo! We've done this kind of writing before. It's so exciting to find answers to our questions. Being an expert feels pretty good!

The next day, Ms. M (as we call her) brought in a bunch of information on our topic: chameleons. When we saw all those books, magazines, and articles, we were ready to dive in.

Ms. M reminded us we can't learn everything about everything about chameleons! Researchers have to stay focused. Our job was to look through the books to find information that answers our specific questions.

She pointed to our chart to remind us what we wondered about the day before. "If these are our questions, what facts should we be looking for?"

That was simple. We said, "Why chameleons change skin color! How their eyes work! How their tongues work!"

"Right," said Ms. M. "We need to stay glued to our questions." She drew three columns on the board. "We are looking for facts in these categories. When you find information, jot it on a sticky note and post it in the correct column on the board. This will help us keep our information organized."

We knew what to do: read like detectives to find answers.

I partnered up with Millie while Ms. M handed out the stickies.

We picked a magazine with an article on chameleons. We read the title and bold headings, like Ms. M has taught us, to see if the article had information in any of our categories. We also studied the photos, diagrams, and captions. There we were, focused like detectives!

And guess what? One photograph showed a chameleon's tongue darting out for a moth. Its caption said the tongue shoots out and captures the prey in a "split second!" "Ha!" I whispered to Millie. "Flash! Goodbye, moth!" She wrote a note and we dashed to the board to post our detail under TONGUES.

tongue catches prey
in a split second

When we hunched back over our article, we found this:
"A chameleon's tongue can be one and a half times the length
of its body." In-cred-i-ble! Can you imagine having a tongue as
long as you, plus another half of you?

Millie and I agreed this was a detail experts should know about
chameleon tongues. Plus, we thought the other kids would go
nuts for this fact! We posted another note under TONGUES.

Sticky notes soon cluttered the board. We read them one by one. Some were in the wrong columns. Some were repeats. (We decided this was actually good because we were confirming our information from several sources.) A few had information that went off topic, like where chameleons live and what they eat. (We set them aside.) When we were finished, we had plenty of details about why chameleons change color, and how their eyes and tongues work.

Over the next few days, during writing time, we looked at websites to make sure our information was accurate. I mean, if you're gonna' be experts, you'd better be sure of your facts. We even watched some short video clips online that showed chameleons changing colors, moving their eyes, and catching prey with their tongues. Then we knew we had our chameleon stuff down pat. Plus, it was amazing to see those chameleons in action!

Boy, were we ready to W R I T E! We tried a few different introductions, but nothing we wrote got us jazzed up. So, we decided to skip ahead since we were bursting with WOWZER chameleon facts! We started with what we learned about chameleons changing colors. We read back over our sticky notes and talked about each one while Ms. M quickly wrote on chart paper. Someone would say one thing, and she'd write it down. Then we'd change our minds, and she'd cross it out. Writing is a messy process! Ms. M says this is good because it shows we are thinking, rereading, and revising like good writers do.

Here's what we settled on:

Chameleons can change the color of their skin. Most people think they do this to camouflage themselves. But that is FALSE! Chameleons are already the color of their environments. They change colors when their mood or the temperature changes. They even change colors to communicate with each other. How would you like to say, "Stay away from me!" with the color of your skin? Chameleons can!

Next we wrote about chameleon eyes. We discovered they have special eye sockets that let them move their eyes in all directions.

Each eye can move on its own, so chameleons can look forward and backward at once! They can see all around them at all times so they stay safe. Can you spot a moth behind you that will make a tasty snack? Chameleons can!

The section about chameleon tongues was pretty easy:

Chameleons have super long tongues with sticky ends. When they spy their prey, they shoot out their tongues. The tongues move quick as a flash. They catch their prey in a split second! Can you catch lunch with your tongue? Chameleons can!

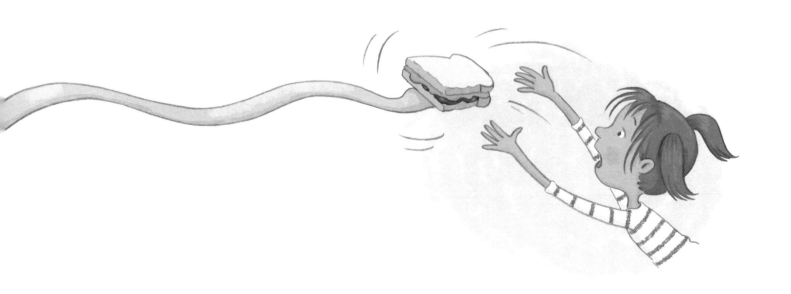

Francesco was so fascinated by the fact Millie and I found, he measured how long his tongue would be if he was a chameleon and drew it on poster paper. He had to tape three pieces together to show the whole tongue!

After working on our writing for several days, we decided it was finally time to write the introduction and conclusion. We studied the beginnings and endings of informational books about animals to get some ideas. One started with a question, so we thought we'd try that.

What animal can change colors, look in two different directions at once, and catch prey with the flash of a tongue? Chameleons can!

We were in l-o-v-e!

"Chameleons can" was like a theme throughout our writing. Chameleons can, chameleons can, chameleons can! What a great intro! It led us right to our conclusion. Ms. M helped us a lot on this one. It's clever, don't you think?

Chameleons are no ordinary lizards. Color change? Check. Look ahead and behind at once? Check. Snatch a bug in a flash? Check. Chameleons can!

You're thinking, that was a ton of work! You're right. But it was also fun. And now we're not just chameleon experts, we're on our way to becoming informative writing experts, too. I'm ready to start investigating my own questions. Hot-air balloons and gymnastics, here I come!

TWO WEEKS LATER

Remember that storybook about chameleons? The one that got our class asking all those questions in the first place? Well, we published our own book, *Chameleons Can*, and put it in the library next to the storybook with this sign:

Got questions about real chameleons
after reading this book?
Who can answer them? We can!

Sharing what you learn . . . that's what informative writing is all about!

Welcome to Stella's world!
I'm thrilled to share Stella's adventures in writing with you.

I've been teaching elementary school for almost 30 years and have loved writing with students from day one. It's just delightful to watch them grow and discover their unique voices on paper. My first goal is always to get students to LOVE writing. But I find that engaging, concrete models of students who love to write are in short supply.

That's how Stella came to life. She's a feisty, intelligent second grader who takes on writing tasks with confidence, employs many useful strategies, and perseveres through the tough parts to get to the writing joy. She's fun. And her stories of writing are fun. Even with increased rigor and higher standards, writing should be fun and purposeful for children. Always. You'll find this to be true across all four of the Stella Writes books. Stella is a powerful mentor and will be a true inspiration for your students.

Stella and her classmates show their inquisitive natures in *Stella and Class: Information Experts*. As their class enjoys a storybook about chameleons, students begin asking lots of questions about real chameleons (page 7). Ms. Merkley (or Ms. M, as her students fondly call her) takes full advantage of this, recognizing their curiosity as an opportunity for shared research. Cherish and celebrate this trait in your students! Encourage them to ask questions, as this can lead to shared research the way it does in Ms. M's class. When a book, video, digital presentation, or other medium inspires questions, capitalize on the moment and have students do research to find answers. Ms. M receives her students' questions with excitement, writing them down and declaring they'll become "chameleon experts" by investigating and writing

about their findings (page 10). Think about how this validates students' thinking. This simple acknowledgment is critical to moving them forward into their own research as the school year progresses.

To further encourage her students, Ms. M brings in a number of chameleon sources but reminds them to stay totally focused on their questions (pages 11–12). She scaffolds this by creating a three-column chart, specifying the categories of information they'll look for as students jot on sticky notes with partners. Creating such a chart is a perfect strategy for keeping students laser-focused and to help them organize the information they find. Partners pay close attention to informative text features (e.g., bold headings, diagrams, captions) to glean important facts about their topic (page 14). Stella and Millie identify two details about chameleon's tongues that they record and add to the class chart in the proper category (pages 14–15).

Soon the chart is covered in sticky notes, and the class is ready to analyze their findings. Then they double-check their facts on websites. Again, this whole process serves as a working model for you and your class as you research a topic. Since this is shared research, you will compose using the shared writing process, as played out in detail on pages 18–26. Just like Ms. M, record students' suggestions and carefully guide them as they cooperatively negotiate what to write. Writing is a "messy process," which indicates a lot of thinking, rethinking, rechecking facts, and renegotiating sentences and paragraphs to get them just right.

Note that Ms. M's class encounters some difficulty trying to come up with an introduction (page 18). They make a few attempts, but decide to skip this portion of their writing and move right into the main ideas or chameleon fact categories. I find this to be a useful strategy when we're stuck on a section of shared writing. Let your students know that it's okay to skip a difficult part and move on, as long as they come back to it later. When Ms. M's class rereads their notes about why chameleons change skin color, they are able to write the first section of their piece (page 19). Over the course of subsequent days, they work out the sections about chameleons' eyes and tongues.

Still needing an introduction and conclusion, the class turns to mentor texts for ideas (page 25). This is a well-known and efficacious strategy. Analyzing the moves of other writers and mimicking their craft often gets the writing ball rolling and can push students over a hump or trouble spot. Ms. M's students are delighted with their solution when they try opening with a question and find the language they develop works perfectly for their conclusion, too. Such is the generative process of writing. As we compose, we discover new thoughts, new questions, and new directions. This is just what happens with Stella's class, and it can happen through the shared writing process with your class, too! Remember, the marked-up piece becomes a beautiful model to hang in the classroom so students can refer to it again and again. After all, writing is thinking, and all the changes are visible signs of that thinking and how it developed over time.

Stella reflects on the amount of effort the project took (page 27), but also on her own learning. She feels more ready than ever to tackle her own questions, bringing the book full circle to the beginning. Just as Stella takes time to reflect, allow students time to process what they did, how they did it, and why. Discuss which parts of the writing process they might be able to take on with partners or independently as they investigate their own burning questions. (It will likely take several shared writing or other highly supportive writing experiences to get to this place.)

The story concludes with the class deciding to share their learning with a broader audience (page 28). They publish their writing in a book and position it strategically in the library next to the story that started it all.* What a purposeful way to celebrate students' efforts! Check with your librarian about making your students' writing available for reading in your library. Your students will be thrilled to think of others enjoying their words!

Stella and Class: Information Experts is just one book in a series of four. *Stella Writes an Opinion*, *Stella Tells Her Story*, and *Stella: Poet Extraordinaire* cover opinion, narrative, and poetry writing, respectively. Writers should have a balanced experience, and Stella is standing by, ready to assist students joyfully as they explore other forms of and purposes for writing!

Additional information for using the books in your instruction is available online at **www.scholastic.com/ stellawrites**. You'll find error-free copies of the texts Stella writes, her pre-writes and drafts, classroom-tested strategies to help students write across genres, and suggestions for using the books with varied grade levels.

I love teaching with picture books, just like students love listening to and learning from them. It's a dream come true to bring a character like Stella into students' writing lives through this medium. I know your students will love writing alongside her! Enjoy!

—Janiel Wagstaff

*Please note: We can't possibly have a real-world purpose for all the writing students do, nor should we. It's critical to write with students daily across the curriculum, as well as involve them in the types of writing covered in the Stella Writes titles. Most of the writing they do should be informal, with only a few projects going through the additional work needed for publication. This notion is explored in depth in the online materials that accompany the Stella series.